# NIGHT DIVE

# NIGHT DIVE

## ANN McGOVERN

### PHOTOGRAPHS BY
### MARTIN SCHEINER AND JAMES B. SCHEINER

**Macmillan Publishing Company**
New York

My thanks to Aquatic Centres, Tortola, British Virgin Islands, for their help and encouragement, and to Lu, George, and Tanya Marler, Simon Smith, Randy and Maritha Keil, and Lauren Cooper

Photographs by Martin Scheiner: pages 4, 9, 12 (top left), 13, 16 (both), 20 (bottom), 21 (all), 24 (top), 32 (top, bottom right), 33 (both), 41 (bottom left and right), 44, 48 (both), 49

Photographs by James B. Scheiner: title page, pages 12 (bottom), 20 (top left and right), 24 (bottom), 32 (bottom left), 36 (both), 37, 41 (top), 45 (both)

Photographs by Ann McGovern Scheiner: pages 12 (top right), 52

Photograph page i : orangeball anemone

Macmillan Publishing Company
866 Third Avenue, New York, N.Y. 10022
Collier Macmillan Canada, Inc.
Printed in the United States of America
10 9 8 7 6 5 4 3 2 1
Library of Congress Cataloging in Publication Data
McGovern, Ann.
Night dive.
Summary: A twelve-year-old girl describes the underwater life she sees while scuba diving at night in the Caribbean.
1. Scuba diving—Juvenile literature. 2. Marine biology—Juvenile literature. [1. Scuba diving. 2. Marine biology] I. Scheiner, Martin, ill. II. Scheiner, James B., ill. III. Title.
GV840.S78M393  1984        797.2'3         84-7163
ISBN 0-02-765710-8

*For Sharon Mulligan*

# CONTENTS

# 1

# GOING ON A NIGHT DIVE

I must be crazy. It's nighttime and here I am on this dive boat, in total darkness. And I'm scared to death.

The sky above me is black except for a half-moon. The sea around me is black. I see lights twinkling on the distant shore. Land seems far away. But land is where most twelve-year-old girls should be. So what am I doing on the sea?

I'm going on a night dive, that's what I'm doing. In just a few minutes, I'll be in that black sea, and it's too late to do anything about it.

How did I get myself into this? By opening up my big mouth, that's how.

Mom and I have been scuba diving on this beautiful Caribbean island for a week now. We've been diving every day. It's been great.

When Jim, who is in charge of diving, first met me, he asked to see my "C" card—my scuba certification card. It proves I've had the proper diving training. You have to be twelve before you can be certified. I went to the local "Y" for my course.

Yesterday Mom told Jim about her work as a marine biologist and about her interest in parrotfishes.

"There are lots of different parrotfishes on our reefs," he said.

Then I blew it. Why don't I think before I speak, like Mom is always telling me to do?

"Really?" I said. "Do you have the kind of parrotfish that spins a cocoon around itself at night?"

Jim grinned. "Sure, kid," he said. "Since you're such a hotshot diver, how about a night dive to see for yourself?"

So that's why I'm on Jim's boat tonight with Mom and the other divers. About to take a plunge into inky waters. I'll probably never even see a parrotfish sleeping in its cocoon. I'll probably be eaten alive by a shark as soon as I hit the water.

# 2

# GETTING READY

"Time to suit up," Jim calls. In dive language that means to get ready. On normal day dives, I'm ready before anyone else. But not tonight.

Jim switches on the boat lights. Mom pats my head. I think she knows how scared I am. She's getting into her special dive suit. Most of the other divers wear rubber wet suits, too.

It's a warm night and the water will be warm, too—about 82 degrees Fahrenheit. On these warm islands, you don't need to cover yourself up for the temperature. Wet suits or shirts and jeans protect you from stinging and scratching coral you might bump into— especially in the dark.

The only thing I don't like about diving is getting ready. There's so much stuff!

You need to wear fins on your feet, so you can move easily without using your arms.

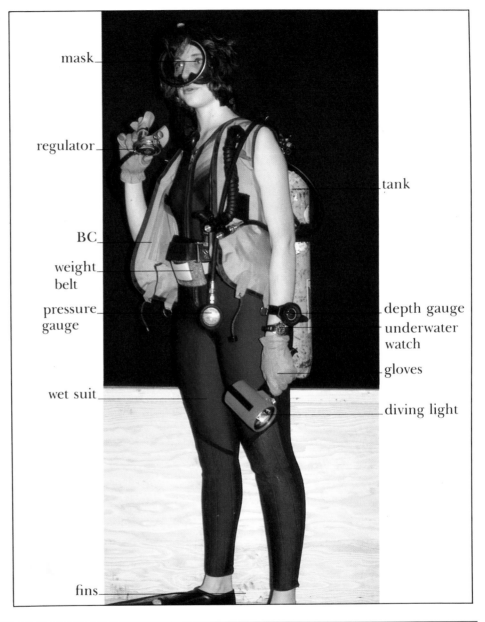

Ready for
a night dive

mask

regulator

tank

BC

weight
belt

pressure
gauge

depth gauge

underwater
watch

gloves

wet suit

diving light

fins

You need a mask so that you can see clearly under water. You need a snorkel only if you want to swim on top of the water.

You need to wear a weight belt, too, with just the right amount of weights on it. The weights help you get down without having to swim hard.

The BC, or *buoyancy compensator*, is very important. It's like a vest and can be filled with air. You can put a little air into the BC and make yourself weightless so you can just float underwater without sinking or rising. If you want to come up, you can put more air into your BC.

The most important equipment is the tank of compressed air on your back. One part of the regulator screws on the tank, and the other part, at the end of the short hose, goes in your mouth. You breathe in and out, nice and easy, as long as you have air in your tank. That's why you need a pressure gauge. It shows how much air you have in your tank. I've always been amazed that a tank is so heavy on land. It weighs more than thirty pounds—but once I'm in the water, I hardly feel it!

Your dive watch shows how long you've been under. And your depth gauge shows how deep you are.

It's a good idea to wear cotton or rubber gloves. You don't want to hold onto strange coral with your bare hands. You may get scratched, and fire coral can sting.

When you go on a night dive, you must carry your own light so you can see what's out there on the reef. Mom has thought of something else, too—light sticks that glow green in the dark. She fastens one to the back on my tank and puts another on her tank. That way, I'll be able to tell where she is at all times. And she'll always know where I am.

Mom is wearing a compass. It's especially important at night to be able to find your way back to the boat.

Jim says having the right equipment is crucial. It makes you feel safer. It makes the whole dive experience easier. You don't have to swim hard or breathe hard or worry about anything not working. Your dive lasts longer when you take it nice and easy and don't get upset.

I look around at the other divers. They don't look at all scared. One couple has been diving for twenty years. Randy has gray hair and a lot of wrinkles. His wife, Sally, has been talking about their new granddaughter. It seems strange to think of grandparents scuba diving!

Then there's Don and his cute girlfriend, Jenny, who is a teacher. Why can't I have a teacher who scuba dives?

There's also Joe, an underwater photographer, who's very busy fussing with his cameras. He's taking a big strobe light down with him. I think I'll stick close to him. I'll need all the extra light I can get. Jim is carrying a big light, too.

Jim makes an announcement. "You've all dived with me before so you know the rules. We'll make a backward entry. That's when you sit on the side of the boat and fall over backwards," Jim explains. "It sounds hard, but it's an easy way to get into the water. Stay close together and stay with me. The boat light will be on all the time. And another light hanging from the boat into the water will help guide you back. We'll enter the water and go down the line. We'll meet on the reef, thirty feet below the boat. Then we'll begin exploring the reef. At some point, I'll give a signal by twirling my light. That means you should all turn off your lights for a minute or two."

Turn off our lights! He's got to be out of his mind. It's bad enough having only a tiny little beam of light in that huge black sea. But to be in total darkness? No way. Not me. I won't do it. I'm leaving my light on all the time.

Backward entry

I sit on the side on the boat. Jim helps me on with my tank and turns on my air.

"Let's get wet," he calls.

This is it.

I look out at the smooth black water, gulp, and roll over backward into the night-dark sea.

# 3

# THE FIRST MOMENTS

I'm in the water, but where's Mom? For a moment, I feel panic rising in me. Everywhere is pitch black, except for the narrow beam of my light in front of me.

Something touches me from behind. A shark? I whirl around. It's Mom. I tell myself to calm down. Mom takes my hand and we start down the line.

Is that the noise of my air bubbles or my heart beating like a drum? My light shows up specks in the dark water as we make our way slowly down to the reef. The specks are *plankton*—tiny creatures drifting through the water.

On day dives, I usually get very excited the minute I hit the water. I just love the feeling of being weightless, like an astronaut— a feeling half like a bird and half like a fish as I swim slowly over the reef or stand on my head.

But tonight I feel only fear. I can hardly tell up from down. The stick of glowing light on Mom's tank comforts me a little.

Suddenly pain shoots into my left ear. Nuts. I was so busy being scared that I forgot to relieve the pressure. I let go of Mom's hand, pinch my nose, and blow out. The pressure goes away.

I look up. The light hanging from the boat is a pale green hazy ball. I see the lights of the other divers below me. I aim mine in front of me. Dozens of tiny shrimplike creatures dance in the beam of the light, like moths around a candle. They are *larvae*, babies of sea animals. When I move my light, they go away. When I keep the light still, they come back.

My fins touch the sandy bottom. It takes only one minute to go down thirty feet but it feels like ten minutes.

I count lights. There are eight of us, including Jim. Jim said we would be able to see the moonlight. He was right. It shimmers on the surface of the water like a pool of light.

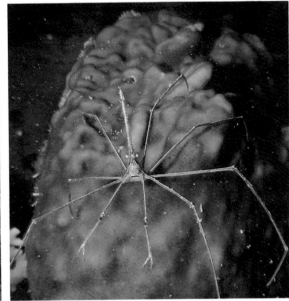

*above:* Spiny sea urchins taking a walk

*above, right:* Arrow crab

*right:* Brittle star

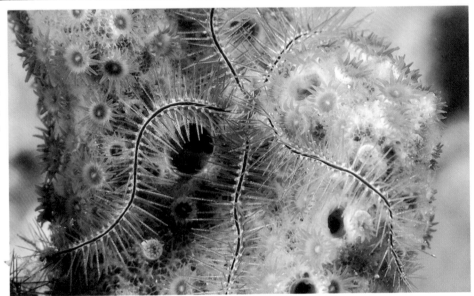

Cup coral with polyps feeding

A strange long tail stretches out on the sandy bottom from under a coral head. The "tiger tail" is a member of the sea cucumber family. Sea cucumbers feed on bits of food and tiny plants called *algae*. I keep my light on it. It begins to shorten, like a huge rubber band.

There are spiny sea urchins everywhere! By day they hide in the coral without moving. I have to be very careful not to step on one. Their sharp spines can jab right through the fins. Tonight, the spiny sea urchins are walking around like pin cushions on invisible feet. They browse on algae. The mouth of a spiny sea urchin is underneath its body. I shine my light on them. In between their black spines, I can see their red and blue bodies.

There's an arrow crab. The arrow crab is just one of hundreds of different kinds of crabs on the reef. It has a pointy head like an arrow and long thin legs like a spider. By day it's a shy creature.

13

But at night it's right out in the open.

And so many brittle stars swarm over the sponges. Each of their five arms moves like a snake and is covered with bristles. They scurry away under the beam of my light. Brittle stars live in sponges by day. At night they creep out to feed. If you catch a brittle star by one of its arms, the arm will break off. But it will soon grow a new one.

On a wall are bright orange cup corals, looking like flowers. The stony coral heads have turned soft and fuzzy.

Hard stony coral is made up of millions of tiny, soft animals that build limestone walls around themselves. The soft animals are called *polyps*. By day, you can usually see only the hard walls. But at night, the little polyps reach out to feed, covering the hard coral with a blanket of soft fuzz. If you look closely, you will see that each bit of fuzz has six little waving arms, called *tentacles*. At night the tentacles reach out to catch plankton. The soft corals of the reef, such as the sea fans and sea whips, have eight tentacles. They feed by day as well as by night.

I start to move away from the circle of lights. Mom pulls me back. Jim has begun his signal. He is twirling his light around and around.

One by one, the divers turn their lights off. I guess I have to now. My heart pounds as I turn off my light.

Now there is nothing but dark. Then little by little I begin to see the shapes of the divers. I move my arm. A stream of tiny stars trail from my fingertips.

Jim begins to swim around us. As he swims, pinpoints of light scatter around his body. The lights are made by a variety of tiny creatures. When they are disturbed, they glow like sparklers and fireflies. There are millions of these creatures in the warm waters

*above, left:* Brain coral—day
*left:* Brain coral—night

of the coral reef. Their glow is called *bioluminescence,* which means "living light."

Night diving. It's still spooky, still scary. But I must admit, it's beginning to be kind of magical, too.

16

# 4

# NIGHTTIME WONDERS

It's so different at night! The fish I see by the hundreds during the daytime are nowhere to be seen. Some fish sleep deep on the reef, deeper than divers can safely go. Some bury themselves in the sand at night. Others fit into tiny cracks and crevices of the coral and hide till daybreak.

The most common night fishes seem to be the red ones—the squirrelfish, the bigeye, and the soldierfish. Their big eyes help them find their prey. During the day I see them hiding under ledges in the coral, watching me. At night, they swim around freely. The little cardinalfish, too, are out in the open.

I see so many new things. My light seeks out a slow-moving trumpetfish. Whenever I get too close to this fish in the daytime, it swims away so quickly I hardly see it leave. But this trumpetfish is sleepy. It's moving very slowly toward the coral reef. It uses its fins as feelers, guiding itself away from the sharp spines of spiny sea urchins.

Here's a sleepy blue tang in its night colors. It has stripes that I never see on a day dive.

I feel a tap on my arm. I turn to see Jim holding a spiny porcupinefish. He rubs it and it puffs up. It looks like a balloon with spines sticking out all over. I've seen porcupinefish on day dives with their spines flat against their bodies. Jim hands it to me. It feels a little squishy. When a porcupinefish is disturbed, it takes in water and blows up to almost three times its normal size. Its eyes are open wide. Its spines are sharp.

The photographer, Joe, swims up to me and begins taking pictures of the porcupinefish. Every time he takes a picture, his underwater flash goes off, blinding me for a second. The poor porcupinefish must be blinded, too. Joe swims away to take pictures of other creatures. I say good-bye to the spiny fish and let it go. It bumbles slowly off into the dark, getting flatter and flatter by the minute until it is a normal-sized fish again.

I see a bright red crab. And more brittle starfish.

Spiny lobsters are out from under their ledges. Their hiding places protect them from creatures of the sea but sometimes not from divers who catch them for food. When I shine my light on them, their eyes glow green. I follow a slipper lobster along the reef. Slipper lobsters don't have claws or pincers. They move quickly over the reef.

Mom and I see a stoplight parrotfish sleeping, wedged tight against a sponge. Parrotfish are large and come in many colors. They have sharp teeth that chomp on coral and help turn it into sand. The mouth of the parrotfish looks like a beak of a parrot and is just as strong.

19

*above:*
Squirrelfish

*above, right:*
Cardinalfish

*right:*
Trumpetfish

*top, left:* Blue tang—night
*top, right:* Blue tang—day
*left:* Porcupinefish puffed up
*above:* Jim with porcupinefish

21

I see a parrotfish with black spots on its side. Mom sees me looking at it and points to a spiny sea urchin. I know what she means. Poor parrotfish—it probably crashed into a spiny sea urchin when it was blinded by a diver's light.

I check my air. How could it get that low so fast? I shine my light on Mom's gauge. She's used up most of her air, too. I look at my watch. It can't be! We've been under almost an hour. It seems like seconds.

Jim swims over and checks our gauges. Then he shines his light on his hand and gives a thumbs-up signal. Other divers are going up, too.

Just think. An hour ago, I hated the idea of a night dive. And now I don't even want to get out of the water.

But in the next few minutes, something terrible happens to change my mind.

# 5

# TROUBLE ON TOP

I start up, feeling good. Feeling really proud of myself because I am no longer scared. Even the dark is friendly.

I see two lights above me. One is hazy green, the other pale moonlight. The hazy green ball of light is hanging from the boat. It welcomes me home.

I'm almost up to the boat. And then I see them! Dozens of little blobs swarming around the boat's light like bees around a hive. I can see right through them. They are transparent, like jellyfish. But they don't look like any jellies I've ever seen.

Jim has seen them, too. He makes a sign that tells us to stop where we are.

What are those blobs? And how long can I stay under while my air is getting lower and lower with each breath I take?

In a flash, Jim swims up and breaks water. Instantly the blobs scatter. He dives down again. He shows us by sign language to put

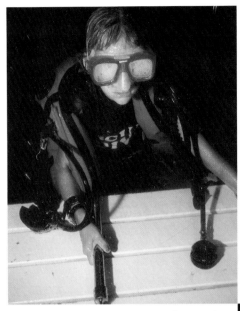

*above:* Escaping from the
sea wasps

*right:* On the wreck
of the *Rhone*

more air into our BCs when we get to the top. That will lift our heads up out of the water.

I'm almost at the surface. The blobs are a thick soup. Jim is at my side. He pushes a button on my BC. My BC vest fills with air and my head bobs clear out of the water. I get so excited that my mask fogs up.

I scramble onto the dive platform. Jim has helped everybody out of the water as quickly as possbile.

All of us are a little out of breath. Jim is the last one to climb into the boat.

"What were those things?"

"Sea wasps," Jim says. He makes a face of pain. "A couple of the little devils got me. Nasty stingers."

He takes a tube of medicine out of his first-aid kit and smears it on his neck.

"I'll be okay by tomorrow. But right now, it sure doesn't tickle," he says.

Jim is so brave. If it happened to me, I'd be screaming and moaning around the boat.

"It's lucky we're not in the Pacific Ocean," Joe says. "The sea wasps there are deadly. They can actually kill."

Oh, great. You won't catch me in the water again with sea wasps—deadly or not. Tonight was my first—and my last—night dive.

Jim looks at me. "Well, little Miss Night Diver, what do you think?"

"I think I'll stay in bed next time," I say.

"Come on, kid," Jim says. "You're not going to let a few sea wasps make you forget the magic of your dive. Sea wasps are rare around here. Chances are good that they won't be around next time we dive at night."

"The next time *you* dive at night, *I* won't be around either," I say.

"Think of what you saw tonight," Jim says. "Think of the crabs and lobsters. The brittle stars and the tiger tail. Think of the funny porcupinefish and the other sleeping fish. The spiny sea urchins and the big-eyed, slow-swimming red squirrelfish."

I think about those things. Slowly the memory of the magic returns.

"Okay, what about diving tomorrow night?" I say to Jim. "After all, you still haven't shown me that parrotfish sleeping in its cocoon."

"We'll start early," Jim says. "Be at the boat by five, everybody. I have a special treat for you."

# 6

# TREATS

We're at the boat by a quarter to five. I wonder why Jim wants us
to start so early. The sun is still shining.

Jim explains. "I said I had a treat for you. It's really two treats.
We're going to make a twinight dive."

"You mean like a doubleheader in baseball?" I ask.

"Same thing," Jim says. "We start diving at dusk, while there's
still light. The light gets dimmer and dimmer while we're under
the sea. We come up in the gloom of half-light. Then our second
dive will be a true night dive."

"What's so special about a twinight dive?" I ask.

"Dusk is a very exciting time on the reef." Jim explains. "That's
when great changes take place. You'll see more fish than you see
by day. Most of them are getting ready to settle down for the night.
Other creatures that hide during the day are beginning to come

out in the open. Dusk is the time for the barracuda and other predators to hunt the reef."

Barracuda and other predators. I shiver. "Does that mean sharks?" I ask Jim.

"From time to time we see a shark or two," he says. "But don't worry. There are only harmless sharks in these waters. Nurse sharks. Small black-tip reef sharks. Nothing more. Nothing to worry about."

I worry anyhow.

Jim tells us the second part of his treat. "We'll be diving in the same place for both dives. We'll be diving on the wreck of the *Rhone*."

Everybody goes crazy with joy. You'd think the wreck of the *Rhone* was covered with gold.

"We've dived on shipwrecks all over the world," Sally says. "But there's nothing quite like the *Rhone*."

Joe has photographed the *Rhone* before. "There's always something new to see."

Don and Jenny, Mom and I are first-timers to the *Rhone*. "I can't wait to tell my class I dived the *Rhone*," Jenny says. Again, I wish she were my teacher.

Jim tells us the story of the *Rhone*. "The year was 1867. The *Rhone* was one of the first iron boats. She was steaming full speed ahead to escape a hurricane when it roared in. High winds and waves slammed the ship onto sharp rocks near the shore. The rocks split the *Rhone* in two. She sank quickly beneath the sea. Today the *Rhone* sleeps on the sandy bottom and fish swim where sailors once walked. Corals and sponges grow everywhere."

"Was there any treasure?" I ask.

"Divers still find bottles and plates over a hundred years old," Jim says. "But so many fish now make the *Rhone* their home. To me, that's the real treasure."

# 7

# THE TWINIGHT DIVE

"We'll make our first dive in the bow section, while it's still a little light," Jim continues. "That's the deeper part of the *Rhone*. We can swim into a passageway right inside the wreck. There are always huge schools of fish in those dark corridors. And if we're lucky, we'll see the huge sea bass that lives deep inside the wreck."

"How huge?" I want to know.

"At least three hundred pounds and twice as big as you," Jim says.

I hope with all my heart the big fish is somewhere else tonight.

"Bring lights," Jim says. "You probably won't need them until you go into the passageways. It's dark there, even in the daytime."

We splash into the water and meet on the bottom. It's not pitch black, but it's not bright daylight either. I'm warmer than I was last night. I borrowed a wet suit from the dive shop.

I think of what Jim has said about the time of the predators. Just

*right:* Fish
in the wreck

*below:*
Spotted
goatfish—night

*below, right:*
Spotted
goatfish—day

*left:* Basket star—day

*below, left:* Basket star—night

as I'm wondering about it, a long silver fish swims by. I can tell a barracuda anywhere by its shape. Its streamlined body is made for speed. Its sharp teeth look deadly. Right now the barracuda is hunting. It darts after a fish. A second later, the fish is gone for good—a tasty tidbit for a hungry barracuda.

Jim leads us down deeper.

Then suddenly there is the *Rhone*, right in front of us. The huge ship looms up in the half-light. It looks so ghostly, so eerie.

There are tons of fish swimming all around. I've never seen so many fish in one place. There are schools of small grunts swimming over the wreck. A spotted goatfish rests on a sponge. Its whiskers, called *barbels*, flick over the sand, looking for food. Already it is wearing its red night colors. By day, it is white.

By day, the basket stars look like tight, tangled balls of straw. I see one beginning to change. The ball slowly opens up into a lacy fan, spreading two or three feet across. The delicate fanlike net catches floating plankton and sometimes tiny shrimp. If I shine my light on a basket star, the end will begin to curl up and soon the basket star will be a tight ball again.

Spiny sea urchins are taking their night walk.

The *Rhone* is not a silent wreck. I hear bubbles and snap-snapping noises. A lot of shrimp snapping can sound like popcorn popping.

Jim leads us deep into the wreck. Now it's pitch black. I twist my light on and gasp.

A huge blimp is in front of me! It must be that giant sea bass. I've never seen such a big fish! Everybody sees it and shines their lights on it. Is the fish getting nervous with eight people around it? Will it turn and crash into us? I swim closer to Mom.

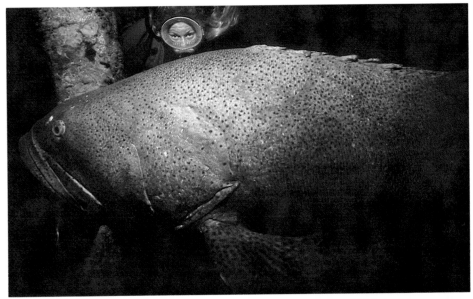

*above:* The giant
sea bass
*right:* Hawksbill turtle

*below:* Fang, a friendly barracuda

Suddenly the sea bass moves away from us. Before I can think of what to do next, it swims out of the *Rhone*, into the darkening waters.

Joe swims after it. Are all underwater photographers crazy?

I still can't believe I've seen it.

I can't believe I'm diving a famous wreck at dusk—the hunting hour!

Back on the boat, everybody talks at once.

"Did you see that little spotted moray eel?" Jenny asks. "Just its head was peering out of its hole." The spotted moray eel is the most common of the eels. It slithers out of its hiding place to stalk sleeping fishes by smell and by touch.

"How about that hawksbill turtle? It seemed to be sleeping already," Don says. "It didn't wake up, even when my light was right on top of it."

Randy saw another barracuda. "It was under the boat as we were coming up," he says.

"That's Fang," Jim explains. "He's our pet. For months, I've been feeding Fang from my hand. Now he comes around whenever he sees our boat anchored above the *Rhone*."

I think about pets. Dogs and cats and turtles, yes. But a pet barracuda? No, thanks.

I wonder if Fang will still be around when we make our second dive.

# 8

# THE LAST DIVE

We have to wait an hour before we can dive again.

Randy and Sally hand out sandwiches. Jim has a cooler filled with cold drinks. Mom has brought apples and chocolate chip cookies.

While we eat, everybody tells diving stories. Oh, the places that Sally and Randy have dived! The Great Barrier Reef. The Galapagos Islands. The Red Sea.

"My best night pictures are from the Red Sea!" Joe says. "I'll show you my pictures of lionfish and flashlight fish when we get back to shore."

Jenny wants to know about them. Joe tells us that the spines of the lionfish are poisonous, so its enemies keep away. The flashlight fish comes out only at night. A patch under its eye glows, flashing light signals to other flashlight fish. The light signals may keep the fish together or help one flashlight fish find its mate. Jim says he's seen a flashlight fish swimming near the *Rhone* at night.

*left:* Rainbow
parrotfish

*below, left:*
Lionfish

*below:* Banded
coral shrimp

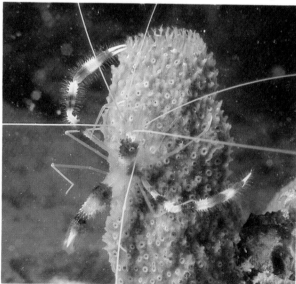

We've already seen three different kinds of parrotfish—the stoplight, the rainbow, and the midnight parrotfish. But Mom is still hoping to see the parrotfish sleeping in its cocoon.

Tonight is our last chance. We go home tomorrow. I hate to think about it. I wish I could dive every night of my life.

The hour passes. Now it's totally dark. We put on our dive gear. When we're ready, we sit on the edge of the boat.

"Who wants to be first one in?" Jim asks.

Something comes over me. I can't explain it. Before I can stop myself, I say, "Me." I turn to Mom, who nods her okay.

Jim grins. "You're turning into a nocturnal creature. A mermaid of the night."

He slips the tank on my back and turns on the air. I check my air gauge. Plenty of air. I put the regulator in my mouth and begin to breathe.

"Over you go," Jim says. "Happy diving."

Before I can change my mind about being first in, I make my backward entry into the water.

I turn my light on, swim to the line, and start down. This time I remember to clear my ears. I look around for Fang, but he's not there.

I feel alone in this vast sea.

But I am not alone. I know there are zillions of fish and creatures below me. One minute I feel very much a part of this watery world. The next minute I feel I'm a lone outsider from another planet. My airtank is my spaceship.

Now I'm on the bottom. I shine my light around. I see the gold gleaming eyes of small shrimp. Some shrimp are cleaners. They pick off and eat tiny animals, called *parasites*, that grow on fish. I see night fish hunting for food. And two dotted snails on a sea

Two flamingo
tongues,
one with its
mantle showing

*left:* Sleeping parrotfish in its cocoon

*below, left:* Lizardfish

45

fan—beautiful flamingo tongues. They feed on the polyps of soft sea fans. The orange and black spots on its mantle look like leopard spots. I get too close. One pulls its mantle back, exposing a creamy-rose shell.

I hear splashes above me. The other divers will soon be down.

I wonder how much we scare the fish and the tiny creatures—the little striped shrimp, the sea stars and the crabs. We must look frightening to them. We are so much bigger.

Jim has warned us to be careful about our lights. He says that if a fish is blinded by a diver's light—even for a moment—it could crash into spiny sea urchins or into a hard coral and get hurt. Fish can't close their eyes because they have no eyelids. I remember the parrotfish I saw with spine marks on its side.

So I try to be careful where I shine my light. I see a red spider star and a crab the size of a basketball. Jim lets me hold it.

And then I see it! A parrotfish sleeping in its see-through cocoon, wedged deep under a ledge. I look up at the divers swimming down. I can tell which diver is Mom by the glowing stick on the back of her tank.

I wave my light. Mom hurries over. I show her the sleeping parrotfish. She hugs me and settles down to study it. I feel I've given her the best present in the world. And it's not even her birthday. Mom has told me that the nighttime cocoon keeps in the parrotfish's smell—and keeps the moray eels from finding it. Jim thinks it might give the parrotfish a warning if an enemy breaks through.

Everyone gathers round to look at the parrotfish in its transparent cocoon. Joe takes a lot of pictures. Then Jim leads us to the *Rhone*.

We're not going as deep this time. Our second dive has to be

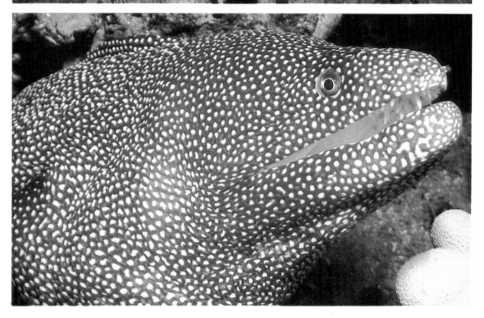

shallow, for safety's sake. So we won't have a chance to see if that
giant sea bass is still inside the *Rhone*.

But I see new wonderful things. A lizardfish that seems to blend
into the sandy bottom. An orangeball anemone. A startled stingray.
The stingray feeds on tiny creatures that dwell in the sand. It will
uncover and scoop a creature out of the sand with its snout. A
stingray will never go after a diver. But if I were to step on a stingray
by mistake, it would defend itself. It might whip up its long tail
with its stinging barb. Ouch!

Suddenly my light goes out.

I see nothing in front of me! Nothing at all but inky blackness.
I tell myself to calm down and swim toward Mom's glowing stick.
She sees my problem and lights up the divers one by one till she
finds Jim. Jim gives me his extra light. Now I can see again.

And just in time. My light shows up a big moray eel. It must be

49

about four feet long. By day, I see only its head and a little of its body peering out from a cave in the coral. Its jaws open and close, showing sharp teeth. At night, eels swim freely over the reef. What if I had bumped into it without my light? How would the moray eel know I wouldn't harm it? It might have thought of me as an enemy and it would have had to defend itself. Maybe it would have bitten me.

I swim away, even though the eel fascinates me. Jim is waving his light around. He's found an octopus. At first it's red, then green. Then it flashes white. Jim puts it on his arm and plays with it. He prods it with the tip of his light. The octopus wraps one of its eight arms around the light. I laugh into my regulator.

Next, Jim captures a squid. He holds it while Joe takes a close-up picture of its eye. Then he lets it go. It jets away, trailing a cloud of ink, the way the octopus does when it, too, is scared.

Though the squid and the octopus belong to the same family, they are different in many ways. A squid has ten arms; the octopus has eight. Squid swim in schools; the octopus is a loner. The octopus can crawl along the bottom of the reef, seeking crabs. When either is surprised or attacked, it can change its color to frighten and confuse the attacker. The squid can become transparent. The octopus changes color rapidly. In these warm waters, the octopus and the squid are small—nothing like the giant monsters I sometimes see on TV.

I feel I want to stay down here forever. There is something new to see around every corner, in every beam of my light.

The coral reef is always changing. In about ten hours, it will be daytime. Creatures who have hidden and slept all night will come out to feed in the bright daylight.

The night creatures will seek safe hiding places. All day, they

Eye of a squid

will sleep or hide. And when darkness falls again, they will turn the coral reef into the strange and magical place I have come to love.

# INDEX